Magnificent
MABEL
and the Rabbit Riot

Ruth
Quayle

Julia
Christians

First published in the UK in 2020 by Nosy Crow Ltd
The Crow's Nest, 14 Baden Place,
Crosby Row, London SE1 1YW

Nosy Crow and associated logos are trademarks and/or registered
trademarks of Nosy Crow Ltd

Text © Ruth Quayle, 2020
Illustrations © Julia Christians, 2020

The right of Ruth Quayle and Julia Christians to be identified as
the author and illustrator respectively of this work has been asserted by them
in accordance with the Copyright, Designs and Patents Act, 1988

1 3 5 7 9 10 8 6 4 2

A CIP catalogue record for this book is available from the British Library

Printed and bound in the UK by Clays Ltd, Elcograf S.p.A.

Magnificent Mabel
and the
Rabbit Riot

My name is Mabel Chase.

Some people say I'm a sweety heart.

Not everyone agrees.

Sometimes life isn't even fair.

Like for instance I don't have one single pet in my whole life.

This is not a good situation because I am keener on pets than most people are.

I know one hundred breeds of

dog and I am up-to-date on the life cycle of a guinea pig.

Pets are better than sleepovers and ice cream.

Pets are my favourite subject of conversation.

Mum and Dad say I am too young for a pet of my own.

They say I am not responsible enough.

When they say this I scream and shout rude things.

Then Dad says, "That's what I'm talking about," and sends me to my room and also he gives

Mum a look over my head that he thinks I can't notice but I can.

I am a noticing sort of girl.

I tell my mum and dad that actually they don't know what they're talking about.

I shout that quite a few people my age have a pet of their own.

I shout that lots of people at my school have two pets.

Florence Carter has so many

pets she can't even count them
up on two hands.

She says it would take her
three weeks to count them.

Florence Carter lives on a farm
in the real countryside.

On farms you have so many
pets you don't even notice them.

Florence Carter has too many
animals.

For example, inside her

kitchen, Florence Carter has got two dogs and four cats and three hamsters.

Inside her bedroom, Florence Carter has a ferret.

Florence Carter thinks a ferret is an everyday sort of pet

when anyone could tell her that
ferrets are rare.

Florence Carter is quite a
spoilt girl.

Florence Carter has chickens
that roam free all day long until
it gets dark.

At dark, Florence Carter has
her own special job of putting

the chickens away so they won't get eaten by a fox.

Florence Carter doesn't like getting the chickens in.

Florence Carter moans about chickens from morning till night.

Florence Carter takes chickens for granted.

But even Florence Carter is not as spoilt as my sister Meg.

That's because yesterday my sister Meg got a true-life rabbit for her birthday.

This is the whole tragedy of my life. Anyone can tell that *I* am the rabbit-y one in this family.

I have rabbit wallpaper and rabbits on my bed and I have a rabbit alarm clock, too.

Everybody knows that *I* am
keener on pets than anybody else
in this house.

Mum and Dad know that *I* am
the one who really needs a pet.

Meg's new rabbit is called
Henry and he has silky fur and a
wooffly nose.

Henry is just my type of rabbit.

When Meg opened Henry's
cage she made a squealing sound.

I thought, Henry is quite scared of that squealing.

When Meg picked Henry up she squeezed him tightly.

I thought, Henry docs not look at all comfortable with Meg.

When Meg looked at Henry she couldn't stop giggling.

I thought, it is quite rude of Meg to laugh at a poor little bunny rabbit on his first day in a new house.

If *I* had a new rabbit for *my* birthday, I would not laugh at my rabbit.

If *I* had had a brand-new rabbit of my own I would keep

an eye on it all day long without stopping.

But my sister Meg only spent the morning keeping an eye on Henry.

After breakfast Meg went to the shops with Dad to spend her birthday money.

She just whizzled out of the front door and waved goodbye.

She had forgotten that she

even owned a true-life rabbit of her own.

When I looked out of the window, I saw that sister of mine skip on top of the pavement.

I saw her smiling at Dad.

I saw her jangle her purse full of birthday money.

I thought, it is unkind of Meg to buy even more presents when she has already been given a real-life rabbit.

I tried to tell Mum about Meg being unkind but Mum was digging the garden and listening to the radio.

Mum told me I shouldn't moan about people when it's their birthday.

Mum said *I* was the one being unkind. "Mabel," said Mum.

"Be a good girl this morning

17

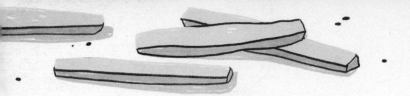

and then we can all eat Meg's
birthday lunch when Meg comes
back from the shops.

"Meg deserves to have a fun
day and she deserves to have a
lovely birthday lunch, too."

I thought, what about me?

I thought, I deserve to have a
lovely day too.

I said some rude things in my
quiet voice that Mum can't hear,

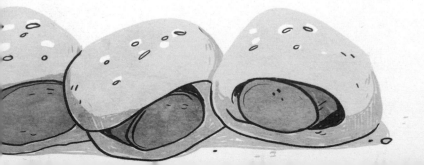

except sometimes mums hear more than you think.

Then I crept over to look at Meg's birthday lunch which was all laid out on the table.

There were all Meg's favourite things and there were some of my best things too.

There were party rings and sausage rolls and salt and vinegar chippy sticks.

There was jelly and cheese
twists.

There was birthday cake with
pink frosty icing.

I didn't even take one chippy
stick.

I thought, I am such a good girl.

I thought, I am not the one who

is spoilt around here.

I left the birthday lunch all neatly on the table where it belonged and I went to have a look at Henry.

Henry was in his hutch and he did not look happy.

I thought, SOMEONE should be keeping an eye on that rabbit.

I could tell in

almost less than a minisecond that Meg was not looking after her rabbit properly.

The only food Henry had was one droopy lettuce leaf.

I thought, that is
quite measly of Meg.

I thought, Meg is STARVING
that rabbit.

So I had to give Henry a
proper lunch.

But Henry did not like party rings, or sausage rolls, or salt and vinegar chippy sticks.

He wouldn't eat jelly or cheese twists.

He would not go near Meg's birthday cake, not even the pink frosty icing.

I thought, Henry is quite a waste-y rabbit and Mum does not like waste one tiny bit.

I thought, Mum would want me to do something about all this waste.

So I invited my friends over for a feast. It was quite a bit fun.

But the thing about my friends is they are messy.

I tried to tell my friends to eat nicely but would they listen? No they would not.

Rebecca dropped biscuit and

cake crumbs on the floor.

Laura-Orla crunched up crisps
in her hand and threw them
everywhere.

Dave was spilly. I was just about to start clearing up all their naughty mess when I remembered Henry.

I thought, SOMEONE should be cleaning that rabbit's hutch.

I thought, Meg is neglecting that rabbit of hers.

So I went to the cupboard under the sink and I got out the green fluffy duster that Dad says is just for cleaning and NOT for playing with, and I used it to clean Henry's hutch.

This was quite a smelly job

because rabbits do a lot of poos.

Luckily, just in time, I remembered that the green fluffy duster is actually a broomstick and everyone knows that broomsticks are too precious to be covered in rabbit poo.

But just when I was about to put that broomstick safely back in the cupboard under the sink, it whisked me up into the sky.

I flew to the top of a rainbow
and slid all the way down. I
landed in the fluffy white clouds.

I whizzed through the air at
153 miles per hour.

But then I remembered
Henry.

I thought, SOMEONE should
be cuddling that poor rabbit.

I thought, that rabbit is
lonely.

So I took Henry out of his
hutch.

But Henry was a bit too
wriggly and he was not very
good at being stroked either.

So I very carefully put Henry
safely in the toy box.

Only this woke up Elwyn and
Bilbo.

They wanted to play the jungle game and, the thing is, they made me join in too.

We swung through trees.

We read stories in hammocks.

We found the waterhole.

I was just getting my breath
back when Meg and Dad came
home from the shops.

Meg raced into the kitchen
and opened Henry's hutch.

Then she looked all around
her, put her hands over her face
and turned to me.

"Mabel," she said all wobbly.
"HENRY HAS ESCAPED.
HE'S HAD A RIOT IN THE

KITCHEN. AND HE'S
RUINED MY WHOLE
ENTIRE BIRTHDAY LUNCH."

I did not say anything.

I thought, what a naughty
rabbit.

Meg looked everywhere for
that naughty rabbit.

Mum and Dad turned the
house upside down.

I searched too because I
wanted to be a good, helpful girl
like Mum said I should be.

I found Henry in the toy box.

Everyone was pleased with me.

They said, "Three cheers for Mabel" and "What a good girl".

They said, "Mabel, you're magnificent."

It was a bit like MY birthday.

Meg put Henry back in his hutch.

She locked the door very carefully.

Then she gave me a hug.

"Mabel," she said.

"Seeing as you were the one who found him, would you like to share Henry with me?"

I looked at Henry's silky fur and wooffly nose.

"That is very kind of you, Meg," I said, "but, Meg, I have slightly gone off rabbits.

"They are a bit too naughty.

"These days I'm more keen on a different type of pet."

"But, Mabel," said Meg.

"I thought you loved rabbits?"

"I do like rabbits," I said.

"Just not as much as snakes."

2

Magnificent Mabel
and the
Burglar Tooth Fairy

People in my class are always
losing their teeth.

Elsa Kavinsky
has lost one tooth
on the top and
two teeth on the
bottom.

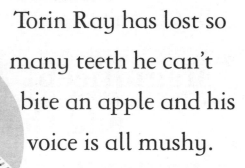

Torin Ray has lost so
many teeth he can't
bite an apple and his
voice is all mushy.

Torin Ray is always asking, "How many teeth have you lost?"

And before I can even answer he says, "I've lost five."

Torin Ray is very keen on the tooth fairy.

But I don't know why he is so keen on someone that sneaks into his room while he is asleep and takes teeth from under his pillow without asking.

That is called being a burglar and burglars are meaner than dentists.

My sister Meg says the tooth fairy is not a burglar because she leaves money under your pillow.

But I don't need money. I have £1.73 already and that is a lot.

I am not planning on losing any teeth. My teeth are good at

chewing and smiling and, also, they're quite good at gleaming.

My teeth are FINE. I am not keen on the tooth fairy.

But then last Sunday at breakfast, something bad happened. I bit into a piece of toast and my front tooth went all wobbly.

I did not scrinch or scream or make a fuss.

I did not tell Mum.

I did not tell Dad.

I did not even tell my sister Meg.

I was calm in a crisis.

Being calm in a crisis is a grown-up thing to do.

Being calm in a crisis is what Dad was when he accidentally

shut Meg's finger in the car door and drove her to hospital without crashing.

But being calm in a crisis is not as easy as it looks.

Especially when you have a wobbly tooth and you are not keen on the tooth fairy.

I stopped nibbling my toast and made a huffy sound and looked at the ceiling.

Dad asked, "Everything all right, Mabel?"

But I did not want Dad to see my tooth in case he noticed it was wobbly so I did not smile back at him.

Mum asked, "Aren't you hungry, Mabel?"

And I shook my head, even though I was STARVING.

Then I got down from the

table and stomped off.

I did not feel calm in a crisis.

I felt cross.

Mum, Dad and Meg looked at each other with their eyebrows up.

They thought I couldn't notice but I could.

I am a noticing sort of person (even when I am stomping).

When I got to my bedroom I looked at my tooth in the mirror

and I tried wobbling it with my
fingers.

It got wobblier.

I thought, I will **NOT** let that tooth fairy get her hands on MY tooth.

I thought, something needs to be done about this wobbly tooth of mine.

I thought, dentists know more about teeth than tooth fairies, and dentists aren't even burglars.

I thought, it's a good job I'm a

dentist in my spare time.

I got my white coat and my dentist mirror and then I sneaked to the playroom and got out the sticky tape that is just for wrapping presents and definitely NOT for wasting.

I thought, Dad says sticky tape sticks everything.

I thought, I'll just use a little bit.

But sticky tape is not really tasty and, also, it sticks your fingers together instead of your teeth.

My fingers would not move.

I thought, this is an emergency.

I thought, SOMEONE should be keeping an eye on me.

I thought, where is that sister of mine?

I called out, "Meg!" in my loudest voice.

Meg came racing up the stairs and burst into the room, all flimmity.

"Mabel!" she said.

"What's the matter?"

"The thing is," I told Meg in my calm-in-a-crisis dentist voice. "I've had a dental injury."

I held out my stuck-together fingers and told Meg what had happened.

"Mabel!" said Meg, all breathless.

"You're not allowed to play with the sticky tape."

"I know THAT," I said, all calm in a crisis.

"I haven't been PLAYING. I do not have time to PLAY.

"I am in the middle of a dentist operation."

Then I stopped being calm in a crisis and got all hot and stampy.

I shouted, "Can you unstick me please?"

I thought, it's a good job SOMEONE in this house has their wits about them.

I thought, I wish Meg would

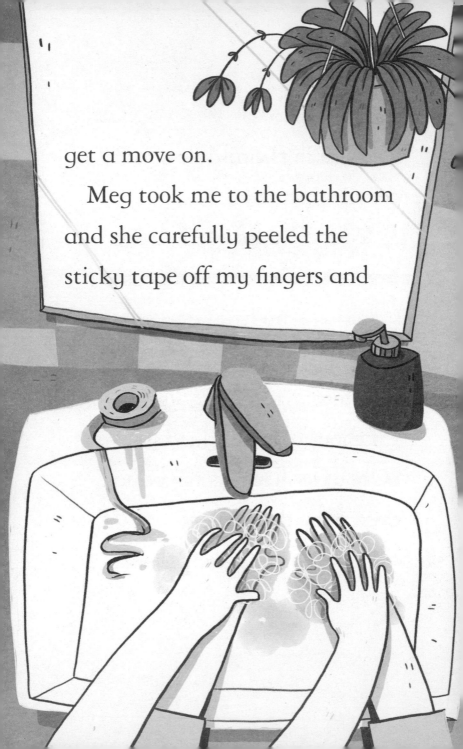

get a move on.

Meg took me to the bathroom
and she carefully peeled the
sticky tape off my fingers and

washed my hands with soapy water.

"Mabel," said Meg. "Have you got a wobbly tooth?"

I shook my head and said, "NO."

I said, "I am not going to lose any teeth because I'm not keen on the tooth fairy and I don't even need the money."

"But Mabel," said Meg.

"When I lose a tooth, the tooth
fairy gives me two shiny pounds.

"Think of all the things
you could buy with two shiny
pounds.

"You could buy stickers
and sweets or you could
even start saving up
for a snake all of your
own."

I thought, I

like stickers and I also love sweets and the main thing about me is that I am very keen on having a pet of my own, especially a snake.

I thought, maybe losing a tooth will be OK.

But then I pictured that burglar tooth fairy breaking into my bedroom and sneaking under my pillow and I thought: NO.

I am NOT losing a tooth.

All that week, I tried to hold my tooth in with my tongue and I stuck to food that was easy to chew, like yoghurt and banana.

But my tooth kept on getting wobblier and wobblier and wobblier.

Then at supper time, when it was sausages, my tooth got so wobbly it FELL OUT.

I thought, why do bad things always happen to me, Mabel Chase?

I put my falled-out tooth in my pocket and I did not tell one single person that it had come out.

Then I wrote a letter to the tooth fairy in fairy code.

Dear Tooth Fairy,

*Please do not visit me in my
bedroom at night when I am all
by myself on my own.*

*Please leave the money on the
windowsill.*

Please go away.

Love from Mabel Chase

I wrote 'Please' and 'Love from' so the tooth fairy would think I was a nice, polite girl, even though I wasn't feeling polite and I wasn't in a very nice mood either.

That night, I put my falled-out tooth on the windowsill and I stuck the letter on my bedroom window.

I lay in the dark for a long

time.

It got very quiet.

Soon it was so quiet, I could hear that tooth fairy flying through the night.

I could hear her breaking into

other people's houses.

I could hear her getting very close to my bedroom window.

I thought, that tooth fairy is a menace.

I thought, why have I been left here all by myself on my own?

I raced to Meg's room and got into bed with her.

In the morning, Meg came with me to see if the tooth fairy had come.

But my falled-out tooth was still on the windowsill and there was no money either.

I thought, that's what you get for writing a nice letter.

I thought, now I'll be tired

and grumpy and it's not even my fault.

But Meg said, "I know what the problem is.

"The tooth fairy only comes if you put the tooth under your pillow."

I told Meg that I couldn't do that because I didn't want to be burgled while I was all alone in my room.

"Well I'm not afraid of the tooth fairy," said Meg.

"You can put your tooth under MY pillow."

I thought, that is very sensible of Meg and it is also a good idea.

I said, "But will I get the tooth fairy money or will you?"

Meg gave me a hug. "You'll get the money, Mabel," she said.

"Because it's your tooth."

And I thought, that is a good point.

The next night Meg put my tooth in a little silk purse and she put the little silk purse under her pillow.

I know this because I checked three times and I made her show me too.

Then I went to bed all happy because I knew the horrible tooth fairy was burgling Meg and not me.

I had a lovely long sleep and in the morning I wasn't tired or grumpy.

I rushed to Meg's room and I

woke Meg up with one jump.

I said, "Can I have my money now?"

Meg rubbed her eyes and she looked under her pillow and she opened the silk purse and inside were two shiny gold pounds!

"See!" said Meg, handing me the coins.

"I told you the tooth fairy was nice."

After breakfast, Dad took me to the shops and I felt all skippy.

"I've changed my mind about saving up for a snake," I told Dad.

"I'm going to spend it all at once on lovely things that I love."

Dad squeezed my hand.

In the shop I chose my favourite sweets and lots of animal stickers and a ball with an alien on it.

But then I spotted a pink princess sticker book and I stopped feeling skippy.

I thought, Meg would like that book and Meg was the one who didn't mind getting burgled by the tooth fairy.

I thought, but it was MY tooth.

I thought, this is just my luck.

I put back half my sweets and I also put back quite a lot of my animal stickers and I picked up that horrid princess colouring book and I took it to the counter.

I glared at the shopkeeper to make myself feel better and I put my tongue through the gap where my old tooth had been.

"Mabel," said Dad when I was paying for everything with my

two shiny gold pounds.

"Are you sure you want that colouring book? You don't normally like princesses."

"I know THAT," I said, because one thing I'm not keen on is princesses, and I don't like colouring much either.

Colouring is TOO NEAT.

"It's not for ME," I said in my slightly shouty voice.

"It's for MEG."

And Dad smiled.

I stomped all the way home and when I got home I stomped around the house until I found Meg.

I handed my sister that measly princess colouring book and then I stomped outside to eat my sweets.

Meg followed me.

She said thank you and she also said that she loved the colouring book.

"Well," I said, "you should love it because it was very expensive.

"It was so expensive that I have no money left."

"Don't worry, Mabel," said Meg.

"When you lose your next tooth, the tooth fairy will give you two more gold pounds."

I didn't say one word.

"Mabel," said Meg. "Are you still scared of the tooth fairy?"

"No," I said.

"I am not SCARED of the tooth fairy.

"I just think she's a bit mean.

"Two gold pounds isn't very much. She should leave three."

3

Magnificent Mabel
and the
Pixie Play Date

I'll tell you what is the most fun thing ever: a sprinkler, that's what.

I don't have a sprinkler in my own garden.

This is why life isn't even fair.

When I ask my dad why we don't have a sprinkler, he says our garden isn't big enough.

But anyone can see that our garden is much bigger than a sprinkler.

When I ask my mum why we don't have a sprinkler, she says the neighbours live too nearby and they would not be

keen about being sprinkled on. But anyone can see that the neighbours would love a few refreshing drops.

When I ask my sister Meg why we don't have a sprinkler, she says, "Come on, Mabel, let's just play in the paddling pool instead."

But everyone knows that paddling pools are not as fun as

sprinklers.

Paddling pools are full of  stones and bits of old grass and they are much colder than the true-life sea.

I know this because I swam in the true-life sea once and it was not at all freezing even though Meg said it would be.

Our paddling pool is freezing and scratching and boring.

Sprinklers are never boring.

Sprinklers are always fun.

Elsa Kavinsky has a sprinkler and Elsa Kavinsky is allowed to play in her sprinkler whenever she wants.

Elsa Kavinsky's garden is bigger than ours.

I thought, I would like to visit Elsa Kavinsky's big garden and play in that sprinkler.

But getting to Elsa Kavinsky's house was quite tricky for me because I am not Elsa Kavinksy's best ever friend.

Elsa Kavinsky is keener on Molly Cooper and she also quite likes Sam Farnborough when he is not eating cheese and pickle sandwiches.

So I had to spend a whole week doing nice things for Elsa

Kavinsky.

I gave her broken crisps out of my lunch box.

I let her watch me do cartwheels.

At lunch break I played her
not-very-good game of chasing
for thirty-four minutes and I
didn't tell her how it could be
better.

Luckily, at the end of the week Elsa Kavinsky asked me over to play at her house.

I said, "OK, I'll come," in a not-very-keen voice because I didn't want to give my game away.

Elsa Kavinsky did not notice my tone of voice.

She is not a noticing sort of girl.

When I arrived at Elsa Kavinsky's house after school I

saw her sprinkler with my own eyes.

It was right there in the middle of her garden.

I stared at that sprinkler until my brain scrunched up.

I said, "Elsa Kavinsky, your sprinkler looks amazing."

Elsa Kavinsky did a grown-up smile and said, "Oh no, ours is only a smallish sprinkler.

Most people have much bigger
sprinklers than us."

This made me want to poke Elsa Kavinsky in the tummy.

But I didn't because I needed to be nice to Elsa Kavinsky so she would let me play in her sprinkler.

I practised holding my temper like my sister Meg has been teaching me.

Meg never loses her temper so Meg knows what she is talking about.

I counted to ten in my head.

I smiled even though I didn't feel like it.

I didn't say one incy mean thing.

But Elsa Kavinsky didn't notice how nice I was being.

She just said, "Do you want to dress up as a princess?"

One thing I am not keen on is princesses.

I don't like dressing up either.

I said, "What I would really like, Elsa Kavinsky, is to play with your sprinkler."

But Elsa Kavinsky did not listen.

She unpacked the dressing-up box.

We played princesses for ages and I let Elsa Kavinsky tell me what to wear and what to say because I wanted to keep her in a good mood so she would take me to play with her sprinkler.

When Elsa Kavinsky got
bored of princesses, I asked if
we could go and play in the
sprinkler now.

But at that exact moment
Elsa Kavinsky's mum said it was
supper time.

We had to stay at the table
for ages because it was spaghetti
and spaghetti is a slippery and
slow thing to eat.

Also, Elsa Kavinsky's mum asked us lots of questions about our day at school.

I don't like people who ask too many questions about school.

School is not a nice subject.

Mums and dads should not talk about school.

After supper there were only ten minutes left before it was time for me to go home.

I waited until Elsa Kavinsky's mum stopped talking (because that is called being polite), and then I said, "Can we play in the sprinkler now?"

And do you know what Elsa Kavinsky said?

Elsa Kavinsky said, "No."

She said, "I'm bored of the sprinkler."

She said, "I don't want to get

cold and wet."

She said, "I want to watch TV instead."

Anyone could see that this was VERY rude of Elsa Kavinsky.

Everyone knows that the guest should be able to decide what to do.

I told Elsa Kavinsky that this was my only chance to play in a real-life sprinkler and that she

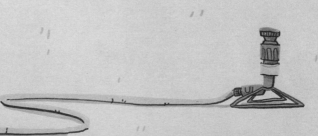

should let me play in it.

Elsa Kavinsky said, "I don't want to."

Elsa Kavinsky said, "I'm tired."

And then I poked Elsa Kavinsky a teeny bit hard in the tummy.

Elsa Kavinsky told her mum.

Elsa Kavinsky's mum's eyes went wide and stare-y.

She said, "I think you are both tired."

She said, "I think watching television is probably a good idea."

But I don't think television is even a tiny bit interesting.

So I decided to think about the

family of pixies that live under the stairs in my house.

The more I thought about
my pixies, the more I started
to giggle because my pixies are
very funny.

Elsa Kavinsky stopped
watching the telly and stared at
me. "Mabel," she said crossly.
"Why are you giggling?"

"I can't help it, Elsa
Kavinsky," I said.

"I am remembering the pixies

that live under the stairs in my house and they are so funny, they make me giggle just thinking about them."

Elsa Kavinsky did not say anything for a long, long time.

Then she said, "Are pixies real?"

I nodded. "Of course pixies are real," I said.

"I have pixies of my own living

under my stairs."

Elsa Kavinsky nodded slowly.

I said, "Shall I tell you all about my pixies?"

And Elsa Kavinsky said, "Yes please" in a sulky voice because she was maybe still quite cross about having her tummy poked a teeny bit hard.

I told Elsa Kavinsky all about the pixies that live under the

stairs in my house.

I told her about the amazing parties they sometimes invite me to.

I described the little outfits that I make for them.

I talked about how their wings
are made out of cobwebs.

I mentioned that the youngest
pixie won last year's Pixie
Olympics for her gymnastics.

I explained that every day I have to tuck those pixies up in their tiny pixie-sized bunk beds and read them a bedtime story.

I said that sometimes the pixies give me a magic lemony drink out of a tiny acorn cup and when I drink that lemony drink I turn into a pixie for a whole morning.

I told Elsa Kavinsky that

pixies are quite naughty.

Talking about my pixies
was so fun and interesting
that by the time my dad came
to pick me up I had actually
forgotten about playing in Elsa
Kavinsky's sprinkler.

I said, "Goodbye, Elsa
Kavinsky. I'm going home to see
my pixies now."

Elsa Kavinsky looked all

concentrating.

She breathed in tight and breathed out again.

She said, "Mabel Chase, you are so lucky."

I said, "I know, I am lucky.

"Not many people have pixies living under their stairs.

"Pixies are VERY rare.

"Pixies are rarer than sprinklers."

In the hall I saw Elsa
Kavinsky's mum having a quiet
word with my dad.

I heard them whispering in
the next room.

On the way home Dad asked
me why I had poked Elsa
Kavinsky in the tummy.

I told him it was not a hard
poke.

I told him it was not my fault.

I explained that Elsa
Kavinsky is not always polite to
her guests.

I said that Elsa Kavinsky is
quite a horrid girl.

Dad sighed.

Dad told me I had to write
a note saying sorry to Elsa
Kavinsky and he also said I
should invite Elsa Kavinsky over
to my house because that is the

right thing to do.

At school on Monday I gave my sorry letter to Elsa Kavinsky and I said sorry for poking her.

Elsa Kavinsky did not notice my fingers being crossed behind my back (because, remember, she is not a noticing sort of girl). She said, "That's OK, Mabel."

Then I had to ask Elsa Kavinsky if she wanted to come

to play at my house after school
and Elsa Kavinsky jumped up
and down like a bunny rabbit
and said, "Yes, yes, Mabel, I
would love to come to your house
because then I can meet your
pixies!"

After that I did not say
anything else.

I was a bit too busy thinking.
When we got back to

my house after school, Elsa
Kavinsky wanted to play with
the pixies straight away but I'm
afraid the pixies were sleeping
so I showed Elsa Kavinsky how
to play my best spying game
instead.

We played for hours. After
that it was dippy eggs for
supper.

Elsa was in a hurry to finish

because she was so keen on playing with the pixies but the thing is, I always take ages to eat dippy eggs.

Dippy eggs are my slowest supper.

Elsa waited a long time for me to finish eating, then she said, all jumpety, "Please, Mabel, NOW can I meet your pixies?"

I chewed my lip a bit and then I sighed like my dad does.

I said, "Yes, Elsa Kavinsky, I'll introduce you to the pixies now if you like."

Elsa Kavinsky hugged me very tightly.

She said, "Thank you Mabel," in a happy voice.

"But Elsa," I said, "the thing about pixies is that they are very, very shy.

"My pixies may not actually want to meet you."

I said, "We'll have to see."